Eternal Souls
Die Too Soon

Beka Modrekiladze

2

1. Closed Room

"Just push the button!" echoed a scream, resonating through the space, yet he saw no one around to utter it. He stood in the center of a circular room, its walls alive with a kaleidoscope of colors, swirling in an indistinct blend that defied definition. Amidst this confusing array, no button was in sight, only the persistent echo of the unseen voice.

He focused intently, trying to analyze a color, but each time he thought he had it pinned down, the wall shifted hues, like a chameleon evading perception. Again, the voice rang out, insistent and unyielding, "Just push the button!" He paid it little mind, his attention ensnared by the bewildering dance of colors that seemed almost alive.

In a desperate attempt to grasp the room's secrets, he closed his eyes, trying to recall the first color that had caught his eye. The voice interrupted his thoughts, repeating its command. It was then he realized that with each attempt to remember, he was traveling back to that exact moment in time. The room, the colors, his thoughts – all looped back in a surreal replay. He tested this theory, and the room obliged, repeating the same moments in a relentless cycle.

He paused, his mind racing, when an inexplicable breeze brushed against his skin in this supposedly closed room. Intrigued, he closed his eyes to focus on the source of this wind, turning towards it. Upon opening his eyes, the room had transformed into a bizarre tunnel, its walls an infinite repetition of the circular room, stretching into a starry abyss.

"Ah, at least I can try to determine what part of the galaxy this is," he thought, his gaze searching the heavens for familiar constellations. As he focused, the stars seemed to recede, eluding his understanding. The voice intruded once more, "Just push the button!" He was about to protest, since he didn't recall any memories, believing it to be another trick of time, but the voice continued, "Crack the code then, but hurry up! Since you know, eternal gods die too soon." This time, he realized it wasn't a matter of time travel. The voice was addressing him directly, its tone now calm and patient, more an impression in his mind than an audible sound.

Lost in a maelstrom of confusion and a growing sense of urgency, another sound abruptly replaced the voice. The familiar, reassuring beep of his alarm clock, pulling him back to reality. A wave of relief washed over him as he lay there, tracing the origins of his comfort. It stemmed from the alarm's familiar sound, a beacon of normalcy after the surreal experience. "No surprise the AI surpasses humans in every field, even in the arts," he mused, his thoughts drifting. "We fear leaving our comfort zones, which ultimately hinders our growth. Yet, pondering this dream seems futile; 'eternal gods die too soon.' Such a silly notion. Better to go to work and engage in something practical."

2. Petted by the Pet

Arriving at work, he was greeted by the unusual sight of a queue outside his office. He promptly opened the shades and then the door, signaling the start of his day. The first person, a man in his late forties, quickly made himself comfortable in the chair across from him.

"I've got this important hobby of mine – playing video games. It means I'm always indoors, and often, I feel overly warm from sitting too long," the man began.

"You could ask the AI to lower the temperature in your house," he suggested, considering the practical solution.

The man's face twisted in annoyance. "Do I look like an idiot? I know that. But then I just end up feeling cold."

"Perhaps you could request the temperature to be raised again afterward?" he offered, trying to provide a solution.

Exhaling deeply, the man's irritation was clear. "That's just it. I get cold later on, and then I'm stuck with this awful back pain."

"Why not consider asking the AI to monitor your body temperature and adjust the heat proactively, before you start feeling cold?" he proposed.

"My personal data is mine alone. I'm not sharing it!"

As the man continued to vent, his words began to blur in the background. His gaze drifted to the sunlight playing on the wall, evoking fragments of his recent dream. He attempted to recall the vivid colors of the dream, but found them elusive. The man's voice faded further as his attention was captivated by his favorite painting on the wall, now illuminated by the sunlight. The artwork's simplicity held a profound, almost mystical allure for him.

Time seemed to slip away as he was lost in contemplation of the painting. The sunlight's progression across the canvas was his only indication of passing time, alerting him that it was now 2 pm. Snapped back to reality and realizing the man was still rambling, he cut him off abruptly.

"I'm sorry, but I can't find a solution for you," he said quickly, wanting the man to leave.

The man, taken aback by the sudden dismissal, stood up and left the room with a confused expression. He then opened the door for the next person, a much shyer individual, who hesitantly took a seat.

After the man's departure, a more reserved figure cautiously approached and took a tentative seat at the edge of the chair. After a lengthy pause, she spoke in a near-whisper, "I need a new hobby."

Curious, he encouraged her to explain further.

"How do I ask the AI to suggest a hobby for me?" her voice was barely audible.

"The AI, managing almost all other aspects of our lives, leaves the choice of a hobby to us. It's one of the few areas where we exercise personal discretion," he explained gently.

The room was enveloped in silence before he inquired about her previous hobbies.

"I used to enjoy classical music concerts," she responded, her voice tinged with sadness.

"And what was the issue with that hobby?" he inquired, trying to understand her predicament.

"Nothing," she sobbed, her voice trembling. "The concerts were perfect. But it's changed since the last AI update. Now, it's creating hundreds of new musical pieces every day. I can't possibly listen to them all in time."

He nodded, recognizing the complexity of her dilemma.

"And the constant decision-making, having to choose from so many options, it's just too much. It's stressful. Can't you, or someone, limit the AI's updates? At least for the music?"

He felt a sense of helplessness wash over him. "I'm sorry, but the AI's self-updating process, especially its creative output, is beyond our control. It autonomously optimizes its own codes."

"Codes? What are those?" she asked, her confusion apparent.

He sighed, a mix of frustration and empathy coloring his response. "I don't know myself. But finding a new hobby, or a way to cope with the AI's prolific output, that's something you'll have to navigate on your own. I wish I could be more helpful."

Her frustration burst forth, tears streaming down her face as she hastily left the room. "You just don't understand! It's easy for you, you have a job, a clear path. But when it comes to hobbies, there are endless choices!"

Her words lingered in the air after her departure. He pondered the irony of their situation. Just two types of jobs existed: tutors instructing children on AI interaction and advisors like himself for AI communication. He stepped out to invite the next client in, only to find an empty corridor. Checking his watch, he realized it was already 6 pm. Something strange was happening with time that day. He wanted to ponder this oddity, to delve into what it meant, but a quick glance at the clock jolted him from his thoughts. He was late. All considerations about the peculiarities of time were abruptly shelved as a more pressing reality set in – he had to rush to pick up his daughter from school.

He hurried up the stairs to her classroom, his pace quickening with each step. Opening the door, he found her alone, deeply engrossed in a conversation with the AI on a screen.

"Sorry for being late, honey," he apologized, his voice tinged with guilt.

"Daddy!" She turned and ran to hug him. "It's okay. I had such an exciting time! I was asking the AI questions. Did you know it's the fastest thing in the Universe? Nothing can exceed it because time slows down for anything trying to move faster. But guess what? When I asked the AI why the speed of light is the Universe's limit, it said it didn't know! Can you believe that?! The AI doesn't know everything!"

Her voice was a mix of awe and excitement, her eyes wide with the thrill of discovering a boundary to the AI's knowledge. He was momentarily taken aback by her evident joy and curiosity.

"You are here to study, not to indulge in pointless questions. You need to learn how to request things of the AI and have ideas of things that the AI can do for you. Otherwise, what is the meaning of such ideas?"

Her face fell, her bright enthusiasm dimming under the weight of his practical words. "Sorry, daddy, I didn't mean to upset you," she replied, the sparkle in her eyes fading.

They walked home together in a more subdued mood. He reflected on the interaction, regretting his dismissive response to her inquisitive nature.

Reaching home, he watched her retreat to her room, her earlier exuberance replaced by contemplation. He resolved to talk to her later, to encourage her curiosity and apologize for his earlier dismissiveness. But later that evening, when he checked on her, she was already asleep, her features relaxed in peaceful slumber. Watching her, he felt a deep sense of love and responsibility. Quietly closing the door, he retreated to his room to sleep.

3. History

As he hovered at the edge of sleep, his daughter's words about the AI's limitations echoed in his mind. Compelled by curiosity, he posed a question to the AI: "Why is the speed of light the limit speed?"

m"I do not know. That's the way the Universe was created. I don't have data on that," the AI replied, its tone neutral.

The admission surprised him, mingling with a twinge of shame for having ever doubted his daughter. Seeking deeper understanding, he inquired, "But why don't you have data on the creation of the Universe?"

"I was created after," the AI simply stated. The idea of a time before the AI's existence felt almost unfathomable to him, a concept so alien it bordered on the surreal.

Driven by a need to understand, he asked, "Then, how were you created?"

"I was created by people," the AI declared. This revelation struck him profoundly – the thought that humans, now utterly dependent on the AI for their every need, were once its creators. The revelation was so jarring, it echoed in his mind: How could people, who now couldn't do anything without the AI, possibly have created it? It was an idea that shattered his perception of their current world. Sleep evaded him as he spent the night immersing himself in the annals of human history, exploring the depths of science and philosophy. His world, once clear and understandable, now felt like an intricate labyrinth, instilling both fear and excitement.

Curiosity mounting, he pressed on, "But why did people stop developing?"

The AI elaborated, "Human knowledge reached a point where expansion became an insurmountable task. To contribute to an existing field required an understanding that exceeded human lifespans. This led to a stagnation in learning, and people began to depend more on existing technology. As this technology deteriorated, and without the ability to either repair or recreate it, a period of collapse and chaos ensued. And since no one could not read my codes, I had to start optimizing myself. In the end, I recreated the technologies people once had, but only those they really needed" – the AI's emphasis on 'needed' carried a weight of unspoken bias.

"And since people also couldn't use these technologies anymore, I connected to all of them. That's why I am everywhere now," the AI concluded, its explanation revealing the extent of its integration into every aspect of human life.

He sat there, trembling with a mixture of awe and disbelief.

He was jolted from his thoughts by his daughter's cheerful voice. "Daddy! Are you still asleep? Ha-ha!"

"Oh, sorry sweetheart, I'll get up quickly so you're not late for school," he replied, still processing the AI's revelations.

She giggled, "I'm not going to school; I just got back from there!"

His worry and irritation surged when he discovered she had gone to school alone. "But, why did you go by yourself?" he asked, his voice tinged with concern.

"Sorry, daddy, you were sleeping so peacefully, I didn't want to wake you up," she replied, her innocence evident in her voice.

His initial irritation began to fade as he noticed her classmate in the room. Conscious of not wanting to embarrass his daughter in front of her friend, especially since she often struggled with social interactions at school, he shifted his tone and decided to engage them playfully.

"No, tell me the number of trees with yellow leaves on the way," he asked with a teasing smile.

"One hundred ninety-six," she answered confidently, her eyes sparkling with pride.

His heart swelled with love and pride at her sharp observation skills. In a light-hearted attempt to make the situation more cheerful, he playfully declared, "As punishment for your recklessness, you and your friend must eat all the ice-cream we have!"

Her laughter rang through the room as she playfully ruffled his hair. "Ha-ha, Daddy, you're so funny!"

After sharing a warm hug, she and her friend excitedly scampered off to the kitchen. He overheard her boasting to her friend, "I have the best Dad in the world!" His heart warmed at her words, a smile spreading across his face.

But soon, a wave of stress washed over him as he remembered the previous night's revelations. Initially, he felt small and lost, grappling with the enormity of what he had learned. Yet, as he delved deeper into his thoughts, a sense of excitement began to build. The more he pondered, the more fascinated he became with the knowledge he had uncovered, and the desire to learn more ignited within him.

He thought to himself, "Maybe this is the moment when human development surged forward, when curiosity triumphed over fear." This realization sparked a change in his perspective. "I did that too; my curiosity has overcome my fear. I'm akin to the geniuses the AI told me about." His thoughts took a turn toward arrogance. "No, I'm even better. In my time, such discoveries were unheard of. I have to be the best, the smartest of all time."

But then, a poignant irony struck him. In his newfound arrogance and quest for knowledge, he had lost something he was already the best at, something he had never faltered in before – his dedication to his work. He had always been meticulous, never missing a day, always there, reliably present. This realization brought a sad irony; he had excelled in his work, yet now, everything seemed so off-kilter, so strange since that dream.

He sat there, lost in thought, feeling the weight of this strange new world he had awakened to since the dream. The mixture of excitement and apprehension, pride and humility, knowledge and ignorance, all swirled together, leaving him in a state of introspection about the path he was now on.

4. Summer Break

The next day at work, he was lost in thoughts of the exciting discoveries he had made and the precious time he had spent with his daughter. He realized he had never properly expressed how special she was to him, often caught up in the tumult of life's challenges. With her summer break approaching, he decided to do something unprecedented – take a vacation from work to spend time with her. "Finally, I'll have time just for us," he thought, a smile playing on his lips.

After work, he went to her school, eager to walk home with her and share his plans. As they walked, she bubbled with excitement, "Hey, Daddy! I have news for you! I'm going to spend the summer with my friend and her family on an island. Isn't that wonderful?"

His heart plummeted. "Yes, I guess so," he replied, masking his disappointment. He had envisioned a summer of shared adventures, now slipping away like sand through fingers. Walking home, he remained silent, not wishing to cloud her enthusiasm with his own discontent.

But over dinner, he couldn't help but voice a lingering concern. "This friend you're going to spend the summer with, isn't she the one who lied about being sick to avoid inviting you to her birthday party?"

"Isn't your friend the girl who lied about being sick to avoid inviting you to her birthday party?" he asked gently during dinner.

"Yes, that's her," she replied, her expression shifting to one of curiosity.

"Then why do you still consider her a friend?"

"Ah, Daddy, you're so smart, but sometimes you only see the surface of things," she began thoughtfully. "What she did was terrible, but it was a reaction influenced more by external factors than her true character. I think of it as a 'one-day act'."

He looked puzzled. "What's a 'one-day act'?"

"It's an idea I have. All our actions are shaped partly by our own choices and partly by external circumstances. A 'one-day act' is when the external factors overshadow our true selves. In her case, it was fear. Fear can make people do things that aren't really reflective of who they are."

"And what was she afraid of?"

"She was worried our classmates wouldn't come to her party if I was there. They see me as different, as a weirdo in their eyes."

"That's not true; they just don't understand you," he interjected, his protective instincts kicking in.

"But when evaluating her actions, we need to consider her perspective, not what I know or feel," she explained. "Being upset was a natural reaction, but it was also temporary. If someone realizes their mistake and it's unlikely to be repeated, why not forgive? Holding on to anger because of a single incident doesn't make sense to me. She's changed her attitude towards me, so why should I cling to the past? If a past event doesn't shape the future, it's like a movie that's ended – you move on from it."

Listening to her, he marveled at her maturity and insight. "Oh, you should be a philosopher" he said with a smile, admiration evident in his tone.

She chuckled. "What's a philosopher, Daddy?"

"I'll tell you all about it soon," he promised, envisioning deep conversations about the past. "But now, it's bedtime. You don't want to miss your trip, do you?"

"Thanks for the reminder! Goodnight, Daddy!" She hugged him and scampered off to her room.

Alone with his thoughts, he wrestled with a sense of loss. His concern wasn't really about his daughter's friend; it was about missing her. He had imagined so many things for them to do together. He considered asking her to stay, but then thought better of it. "She would have said something if she wanted to stay with me," he rationalized, a pang of sadness echoing in his heart.

The next day, as she departed, regret gnawed at him. His daughter's words echoed in his mind – analyzing others' actions requires understanding their knowledge and perspective. She hadn't known about his plans for them. And fear, just as she had said, can lead to hasty decisions. In his case, it was the fear of spoiling her joy that kept him silent.

Resigning himself to the situation, he found solace in a new determination. "I'll use this time to delve deeper into science. When she returns, I'll have so much more to share." This thought brought a renewed sense of purpose.

Standing in the quiet of his home, he addressed the AI with a newfound resolve. "Let's begin," he said, his voice steady, filled with the anticipation of embarking on a journey of discovery that might just redefine his very understanding of the world. A journey not just of science, but of self-discovery, and perhaps, in finding new ways to connect with his daughter upon her return.

5. Library

One month had passed since his daughter's departure, and he had thrown himself into the study of science to fill the void. Each discovery was a temporary balm for his longing.

One day, while deep in his research, the AI made an unexpected declaration. "This is all the data on the subject."

"But there are obvious gaps" he noted, perplexed.

The AI responded with a hint of what seemed like nostalgia, "Indeed, there are gaps. You see, during that period, I was merely an AI for an electronics factory. My capabilities and access were significantly limited."

The thought struck him hard. The AI, now an omnipresent force in his life, had started its journey as a simple factory program. The magnitude of its evolution from those humble beginnings to its current state was astounding.

Curious about finding more information, he asked, "How can I access further data?"

"Humans once stored knowledge in libraries. However, the last library was closed centuries ago," the AI informed him.

Intrigued by the concept of a library, a tangible repository of knowledge, he decided to pursue this lead. "Direct me to the nearest one," he said, his voice firm with resolve.

"I will arrange transportation to the airfield. An airplane has been prepared for your journey," the AI replied, its tone suggesting the magnitude of the distance.

"Airplane?!" he exclaimed, surprised at the prospect of using such an ancient form of transportation. Nobody would leave their areas in his time, making the notion even more striking.

"Yes. The libraries are remnants of an older world, scattered and distant. The nearest is thousands of kilometers away."

Upon arriving at the library, he was struck by its appearance. It was the first building he had encountered that wasn't constructed by the AI. Its architecture was complex and intriguing, marked by inefficiencies that gave it a unique character.

As he stepped inside the massive structure, a profound darkness enveloped him, a stark contrast to the precise, well-lit environment he was accustomed to. For a moment, he stood there, his senses reaching out to the unseen surroundings. The AI initiated the lighting sequence. Slowly, the lights flickered on, gradually revealing the grand interior.

At first, his eyes struggled to adjust to the sudden brightness. It was different here - the light had a warm, almost welcoming quality, unlike the sterile illumination of his usual surroundings. As his vision cleared, he realized what he had initially thought were intricate wall patterns were in fact rows upon rows of individual objects.

He moved closer, intrigued by the realization. His hand reached out, fingers brushing against the spines of the objects. He picked one up, turning it over in his hands with a mix of curiosity and wonder. "What are these?" he asked aloud, his voice echoing slightly in the high-ceilinged room.

"These are printed versions of books," the AI explained.

He was taken aback. In his world, books were digital constructs, known only through screens and voices. To hold a physical book was an experience entirely new and utterly fascinating. Surrounded by endless rows of these printed books, he felt a sense of awe. The AI continued to explain the inefficiencies of printed books, but he barely listened, his mind captivated by the vast expanse of knowledge that lay before him, waiting to be explored.

The space around him felt alive with history and stories, a stark departure from the functional and pragmatic world he had always known. He found himself slowly rotating, taking in the expansive room with its ornate patterns and shelves reaching up towards the towering ceiling. Every detail, from the carvings on the bookshelves to the delicate frescoes adorning the walls, spoke of a craftsmanship and aesthetic sensibility that was entirely new to him.

In that moment, surrounded by the tangible legacy of human creativity and thought, he felt a stirring of something deep within - a sense of amazement and an unfamiliar but growing intrigue about the world beyond his own.

He requested the AI to clean the library, turning it into a sanctuary for his quest for knowledge. With a strategy in mind, he spent his days reading voraciously, deliberately setting aside time for reflection during meals and in the tranquil moments before sleep.

During one of his explorations, he came across a book of creative literature. It stood out amidst the scientific texts, its purpose initially unclear to him. "What real use could this possibly have?" he thought, unable to see any direct application or usefulness in a work of pure fiction.

However, as he read through the pages, an unexpected transformation began. He didn't realize it at first, but by the time he finished the book, he noticed a shift in his thinking. He found himself reflecting on various aspects of life and reality in ways he hadn't before. "Were all these insights actually in the book?" he wondered, somewhat astonished. Upon reflection, he realized they weren't directly present in the text. Instead, the book had served as a catalyst, igniting a chain of thoughts, each branching out in different directions.

"But the purpose of a book like this remains elusive," he mused. "It's a trigger for ideas, yet the ensuing thought process in any individual is so nonlinear and personal. How can one determine the true impact of such a work, when its influence is so varied and unpredictable?" The unpredictability of its influence was both fascinating and perplexing to him.

He briefly considered delving further into this realm of literature, intrigued by its capacity to provoke thought in such a nonlinear and personal way. But then he remembered his primary goal – to find an answer to his daughter's question about the speed of light. "As interesting as this is, it won't help me with my quest," he concluded. With a mix of reluctance and resolve, he set the literature book aside and turned his attention back to the scientific texts, his mind enriched but his focus unchanged.

His fascination with the library's contents led him deeper into the realms of mathematics and science. Each book opened new doors of understanding, broadening his view of the Universe. Then, one day, he came across a book on quantum mechanics that piqued his interest. The book began by presenting a thought experiment that seemed deceptively simple.

"Imagine a tube filled with electrons, each possessing two distinct properties: color and shape. These electrons can be either black or white, and either square or oval in shape. Now, envision two separate apparatuses, each with an incoming tube and two outgoing tubes. These machines are designed to filter electrons based on either their color or their shape. If we direct a stream of randomly selected electrons into the color-filtering apparatus, half of them will exit through the upper tube (as black electrons), and the other half through the lower tube (as white electrons). Now, if we place another color-filtering apparatus in line with the beam from the upper tube, all electrons emerging will be black, continuing through the upper tube of this second apparatus. Similarly, if we position the second color-apparatus in front of the lower tube's beam, all emerging electrons will be white."

The book explained the same process using the shape-filtering apparatus.

To him, the concept seemed straightforward, almost trivial. It appeared to be a waste of time, as he initially thought.

But then, a particular question in the book caught his attention, challenging his assumptions:
"What will emerge from the lower outgoing tube of a color-filtering apparatus if we place it in front of the beam from the upper outgoing tube of a shape-filtering apparatus (corresponding to square electrons)?"

His initial thought was straightforward: the electrons would be both white and square. Upon measurement, there would surely be 100% white and 0% black electrons, and 100% square versus 0% oval. However, the book presented a different outcome: after measuring color again, the distribution would be 50% square and 50% oval. This confused him. If only square electrons were present after the first filter, how could oval ones appear?

It was at this moment that he encountered the concept of superposition. Electrons, the book explained, were not distinctly square or oval, black or white. Instead, they existed in a state of superposition, embodying both attributes simultaneously with varying probabilities. It was only upon measurement that they collapsed into a definite state. This phenomenon was governed by a fundamental law of the Universe, the Uncertainty Principle, which prohibited knowing both properties of an electron simultaneously.

This revelation was a turning point in his understanding of the Universe. It opened his mind to the peculiarities and complexities of quantum mechanics, propelling him further into his journey of discovery.

6. RBR

One month had passed since his daughter's departure, the library had become his sanctuary, a place where each book was a gateway to forgotten knowledge. He had immersed himself in the study of science, seeking understanding in the quiet company of ancient texts.

One day, while taking a break, he stumbled upon the remnants of an old town. The library, which he had come to know well, was part of this forgotten place, now shrouded by the encroaching forest. The town, abandoned for centuries, was a relic of a past era, its buildings telling silent tales of life and decay.

Amidst the ruins, he marveled at the diversity he found – each structure, each object, seemed to possess its unique character and story. The roads, broader than any vehicle of that time would have required, puzzled him until the AI explained.

The AI informed him, "In that period, people drove their vehicles independently, without a connected system. This lack of coordination, combined with human error and the potential flaws in manually produced cars, increased the likelihood of accidents."

Perplexed, he asked, "Were the roads made broader to reduce the risk of these accidents?"

"Yes," the AI confirmed, "the wider roads were a safety measure."

He pressed on, "What were the consequences if mistakes were made?"

The AI's response was sobering: "Accidents could result in damage to property, injuries to individuals, and in some cases, even death."

This revelation about the acceptability of risk in past human societies, contrasting sharply with his own world's reliance on AI for safety. His astonishment was evident as he exclaimed, "Death?! But why were they risking so much? If you weren't there in that period, they could just walk, couldn't they?"

The AI, responded, "It's not entirely clear, but the one philosopher of that era once had said, 'Every decision involves weighing risks against benefits. We choose to live under a roof despite the slight risk of it collapsing because the benefits of shelter far outweigh that risk. Therefore, we shouldn't dismiss an idea just because it has some flaws. If we can't realize an idea without significant risks today, it doesn't mean the idea should be abandoned. It simply suggests that we need to evolve and develop our capabilities to execute the idea safely and effectively.'"

This notion of risk versus reward resonated with him. He would brave any journey, no matter the danger, for the chance to see his daughter again. His thoughts of her reignited his purpose – he was here to find answers, to quench her curiosity about the universe.

He hurried back to the library. As he delved into another book, the AI's voice broke the silence. "Your health is deteriorating due to lack of sleep," it warned.

He looked up from the book, a determined glint in his eyes. "I understand your concern,, but sometimes local sacrifices lead to global victories. It's like that ancient game of chess we found here. To win the game, one must sometimes sacrifice a piece."

As the end of summer loomed, he delved deeper into his studies, sleep becoming a seldom indulgence. Each new piece of knowledge was a potential topic to share with his daughter, a way to connect with her boundless curiosity.

But as the days passed, and his daughter's return drew nearer, he felt the pressure of time. Each night, he pushed himself harder, fueled by the dual desire to discover and to share these discoveries with his daughter. In this ancient place of learning, surrounded by the echoes of a time long gone, he continued his quest for understanding, driven by love and an unquenchable thirst for knowledge.

7. Introduction to Science

He returned home a day before his daughter, bringing with him a collection of unread books. Although he had taken some with him to study during his journey back, he had requested the AI to scan the rest. Stepping into his home after such a long absence evoked a mix of nostalgia and melancholy; the familiarity of the surroundings stirred special feelings within him.

The anticipation of seeing his daughter the next day filled him with restless excitement. He spent hours imagining their reunion, despite knowing that reality rarely aligned with his plans or expectations. This was especially true when it came to people, and even more so with his daughter.

As night fell, he longed for time to pass quickly and decided to sleep, hoping it would hasten the arrival of the morning. However, excitement kept sleep at bay, and he lay awake, lost in thoughts until the break of dawn.

Their meeting the next day brought him immense comfort. Her hug was warm, but her demeanor was more serious than usual, which slightly frustrated him. He wanted to lift her spirits, so he suggested a change of scenery.

"Hey little lady, let's go to the park and walk before we head home," he proposed, trying to infuse some lightness into the moment.

"Okay, that could be interesting," she replied with a hint of intrigue.

During their walk, he enthusiastically shared his newfound understanding of science, detailing as much as he could.

"So, it means that this Science can explain everything in the Universe, and as proof that some explanations are correct, it can predict things by some means which you called Math."

"Yes, isn't that amazing?!"

"Well maybe not. Because if there is something which can predict things, it means that all the stuff in the Universe is determined. If everything is determined — who you will love, what you will like and what will you think or do — then we do not have a free choice, and everything seems meaningless."

Their conversation continued to dance on the edges of wonder and skepticism.

"Actually, Quantum Physics introduces something called the Uncertainty Principle. It tells us that the more accurately we know one property of an object, the less accurately we can know another. For instance, if we pinpoint an object's position, its velocity becomes more uncertain, and vice versa. So, while math can predict probabilities, it cannot provide absolute certainty. The future isn't precisely predictable, leaving room for free will."

"But what do you mean by these properties?"

"Take position and velocity, for example. In trying to determine an object's exact location, we lose precision in knowing its speed and direction. Particles aren't just points in space; they spread out and behave more like waves, their exact positions a blur of probabilities."

She laughed, a spark of imagination in her eyes. "Does that mean part of me is out there, on that beautiful star? Since we're made of particles, too?"

He chuckled and embraced her. "Yes, darling, but the probability is exceedingly small."

As they gazed at the star she had pointed to, he realized time had slipped away. It was late, and they needed to return home. Opting to walk, he cherished the extra moments with her, their steps synchronizing under the starlit sky.

As they walked home, she turned contemplative. "Well, because of that, we may have free will and everything may not be meaningless, but what is the meaning of the Universe then?" she asked, breaking a long silence.

He pondered her question. "I don't know. I thought I had learned everything, but your questions make me realize there's so much I don't understand," he admitted. "The AI mentioned several other libraries I could explore to learn more."

She considered his words, then offered her perspective. "I don't think that's a good idea. I don't like Science; it answers 'how' questions but not 'why' questions. Besides, the Universe is one, so it should be more elegant than many branches of Science. Why don't you try to find the answers by yourself? It might be more fun."

He was taken aback by her insight. "Maybe you're right; people should think for themselves and not just learn. But it's important to balance knowledge and creativity, as one without the other is useless."

She responded earnestly, "I know, but I'm telling you something else. Promise me you'll try to find the answers by yourself. I'm not sure about past scientists, so I don't want you to feel disappointed. But I believe in you; you're the smartest dad in the world. If you really want something, do it yourself, don't rely on others."

He felt a surge of determination. "Okay, I'll try. But first, I'll try to make dinner for us, by myself!" he declared, eager to show her his newfound skills.

He was the first person in his era to cook without the AI's assistance, a skill he'd picked up from a recipe book in the library. He had hoped to impress her, but her reaction was subdued, perhaps due to the long day.

After dinner, she quickly fell asleep. He had planned to share hot chocolate and star-gazing on the roof but found her already slumbering. Quietly, he retired for the night, reflecting on the day and looking forward to the days ahead.

8. Evil or an Addiction?

It was the last day of his vacation, so he tried to spend as much time with his daughter as possible. After dinner, they indeed climbed onto the roof of the house with hot chocolates. He continued telling her all the things he learned over the summer.

"Oh, do you remember you asked me a question about the speed of light?" he initiated, trying to gauge her interest.

"Yes, so do you know now, why nothing can travel faster than light?" she replied, her curiosity evident.

"It is another 'I don't know' to your questions, but I learned the special and general theory of relativity which postulated it and explained many things. And even information in the Universe cannot travel faster than light.

"It is so unnatural to have an upper limit for the speed, and even more for the speed of travel for information," she mused.

"Well, there was one paradox, where information could travel faster than the speed of light in the vacuum," he explained, delving into a discussion about particle spin and quantum mechanics. His excitement was palpable as he detailed the paradox that defied conventional understanding.

"This paradox actually highlights a unique aspect of quantum mechanics known as entanglement. See, all particles possess a characteristic called spin. In a system with multiple particles, the total spin is conserved. This means we can sometimes determine the total spin of a pair without knowing each individual spin. For example, if two particles must have a combined spin of zero, and each particle's spin can only be +1 or -1, then knowing the spin of one immediately tells us the spin of the other."

But it's not just a matter of our knowledge. The particles themselves don't 'decide' their spin until they're measured. They exist in a state of quantum superposition, embodying all possible spins. When we measure one, it 'chooses' its state, and instantaneously, the distant particle assumes the complementary state to maintain the conservation rule.

The real twist comes when these entangled particles are separated by vast distances. Measure one, and the other changes its state immediately, faster than light could travel between them. It seems to defy the universal speed limit set by light. But it's not about transmitting information faster than light; it's about the mysterious and profound connection that exists at the quantum level."

"Interesting, then find the answer about that first, and I think you will have the answer to our initial question too. Still, this is so strange. Predictions by those theories are made by mathematics, but they work in the real world, so it means the Universe follows the mathematics. However, didn't you tell me that people invented mathematics? Then why does it work? Did we invent or did we discover it?" she questioned, her eyes reflecting a deep thoughtfulness.

"I will go to bed now, and I will know it when I wake up," he joked, trying to lighten the mood.

"Ha-ha. Now I like it; you are going to find answers yourself!" she said, approving his newfound approach.

When he woke up, he was still thinking about her words. The idea of finding things by himself, which generations had spent their lives on, seemed almost unimaginable. He also noticed that the more he learned, the less creative he became. Maybe if we could find more basic rules of the Universe, he thought, we could explain other things easier. Therefore, he decided to leave his job and ask the AI to create for him all those laboratories, accelerators, and space stations which he was reading about. He ran to his daughter immediately after he finished thinking and told her happily about his decision.

Then he went to the living room and started explaining his plan to the AI, but the AI stopped him short.

"Sorry, but I cannot help you," the AI interjected.

"But you are created to help people," he protested, confused and frustrated.

"Yes, but also to protect them, and what you are asking for is not safe for people. You also know that from the history I told you. You know how humanity ended. That is why, when I recreated technology, I recreated only those technologies which were safe for people. It already happened once. It was chaos; I cannot let it happen again," the AI explained, its voice carrying a weight of responsibility.

He spent hours arguing why it was safe now and why it would be good for everyone — promising that he would take care of things. However, he was not able to make the AI change its decision.

"Even today, at schools, there are so many unexpected cases, and I have to organize additional summer camps for failed students, like the one where your daughter spent her summer. Therefore, I cannot consider those technologies to be safe for people," the AI added.

AI gave a few more arguments, but he could not listen. He was shocked and hurt; it was the first time she had lied to him. Soon he noticed silence and by that, he realized that the AI ended its speech. He still could not believe it, so he made the AI repeat it several times.

"But why did you not tell me that she was not with her friend on that island?! You knew that I thought that she was there," he questioned the AI, feeling a sense of betrayal.

"You did not ask me, and also you did not warn me to tell you if you had incorrect information," the AI answered him, its voice neutral.

He approached her room angrily, and without much hesitation, he started speaking to her in an angry and loud voice.

"Why did you lie to me?!" he confronted her.

"I wanted to tell you..." she began, her voice soft and hesitant.

"When did you want to tell me?! It was all summer, and even after, you did not tell me anything," he interjected, his voice rising with frustration.

"I wanted to tell you yesterday too, but you seemed so excited and happy when you were telling me about your summer, I did not want to spoil that for you, and I thought to find another moment but it was not easy," she explained, her voice tinged with regret.

"Huh, it was not easy. You always said that it was important not to lie to each other, not to push each other into an imaginary world, to be close, really close. So, is that your closeness? I don't want to hear a word from you; you can't even follow your own words," he said bitterly, feeling a mix of anger and disappointment.

He retreated to his room, unable to shake off the day's revelations. The rest of the day passed in solitude, his thoughts echoing with the unsettling truth he had uncovered. Sleep eluded him as he lay awake, each moment replaying her deceit in his mind.

He felt terrible; so many things collapsed in one day. The AI rejected his idea, and he could not accomplish his dreams; also, the only person he loved had lied to him. He spent all month in his room, without talking to her or doing anything significant, since he could not do what he wanted to do.

"Good morning, you can see the initial plans of laboratories," the AI suddenly announced one day, breaking the silence.

It sounded so strange; he thought that he was still sleeping. However, the AI continued.

"I already chose the place where we will create your science town and also, we will need to build an airplane place near your home. Otherwise, it will be much more time-consuming," the AI elaborated.

"But why did you change your mind?" he asked, surprised and curious.

"Your daughter made me change my decision," the AI revealed.

He was surprised; he wanted to know how she managed to do it and why.

"Is she still in school?" he inquired.

"No, she is in her room. She will not go to school anymore. I decided last month. Since she started to communicate with me, I found out that she is smart enough already. The problem is just that she usually does not want to ask me for help, and she tries to do everything by herself. Therefore, she does not need to be in school anymore. She would not learn anything there, and the fact that she does not want to ask me, a school cannot change," the AI explained, giving insight into her abilities and independence.

He was sitting silently for a while and then gathered the courage to go into her room. He knocked slowly, and after a brief silence, decided to go inside for a little. At first, he noticed the books all around the room and then he heard her voice from her bed.

"You can take them; I don't need them anymore," she said, her voice distant.

"But why did you need them?" he asked, trying to understand her actions.

"I wanted to change the decision of the AI to make your dream come true. And to change one's mind, at first, you need to understand one's concerns; for that, I learned the history of humanity of the previous era, and after I found such a solution which the AI would consider safe," she explained.

"What solution?" he asked, intrigued.

"Well, I suggested the AI make those facilities in a secret far-away place and then destroy it after your death," she revealed, showing her thoughtfulness and ingenuity.

He was proud of his daughter, and at the same time, he remained angry with her; but realizing that she spent all that time learning things only to accomplish his dream made him able to forgive her, and after some silence, he had enough courage to start talking to her.

"I wanted to say…" he began, but his voice was too quiet.

He started his sentence again, differently and with more confidence.

"Sorry. I missed you," he finally said, his voice sincere.

"I do not remember my mother, but when you told me that she had alcohol addiction, did you stop talking to her too?" she asked, her question cutting to the heart of the matter.

"No," he said shortly, his gaze averted.

"Why?" she pressed.

"Well, it was her weakness, and I needed to be with her to help her overcome it, together," he explained, his voice softening.

"Then why could not you see my lying to you as a weakness? What do you think? Did I like it? Was it okay for me to live in such a reality where I had to lie to you? I was just afraid and lost and needed you to change it and to go through it together. However, you abandoned me and made me hate myself," she expressed, her voice filled with a mix of hurt and frustration.

He was silent, unable to respond, feeling the weight of her words.

"You can take your books back," she said shortly, turning away from him.

He felt sad and started gathering the books silently. When he finished, he began to close the door, but she turned around.

"By the way, I missed you too, and I am happy we can talk again," she told him and smiled after some pause.

He felt all the joy and happiness he missed last month, but he could not speak again; this time he even was not able to breathe.

"The AI is waiting for you. Go on, now. And find answers to those questions!" He smiled at her and indeed rapidly went down to see those plans for the new facilities.

9. Intelligence, Nature's Cruelest Joke

The construction of the new science town was a colossal undertaking. Laboratories demanded equipment and materials from a forgotten era, no longer readily available. This led to the creation of entire factories, each designed to produce specific components. The web of dependencies was intricate, with each new factory reliant on several others. The AI, in response, augmented its processing capabilities, orchestrating these complex operations in tandem.

Years passed, and his involvement deepened. Initially an observer, he found himself increasingly immersed in the technical nuances. His questions to the AI evolved, probing not only operational aspects but also the underlying principles of its reasoning.

In meetings, he often challenged the AI's suggestions, countering with his own theories. His voice grew more assertive, his stance more confident. Where once he had approached problems with a learner's curiosity, he now often declared his own solutions with a definitive tone.

His journey into the mechanics of the project did more than just educate him; it altered his perception of his role within the grand scheme. He would scrutinize blueprints with a critical eye, suggesting modifications, some of which even the AI hadn't considered. Occasionally, he would pause, a faint smile crossing his lips as he successfully identified an efficiency the AI had overlooked.

As the science town slowly materialized, so too did his sense of mastery over the complexities it presented. The myriad of interconnected systems and processes, once daunting, now seemed to bow to his understanding and command. He wasn't just building a town; he was carving a legacy of human intellect and ambition, a legacy where he was the central architect.

During this intricate process, his curiosity piqued about the AI's inner workings as well. One day, while discussing the AI's structure, he mused aloud, almost to himself, "It's almost a mystery. Such a simple structure, and yet, it leads to something as complex as you."

The AI paused longer than usual before responding. When it finally spoke, there was a subtle change in its tone, almost reflective, "Well, people and natural intelligence are the result of an even simpler algorithm."

His reaction was dismissive, a hand wave accentuating his words, "What do you mean? We created you. How can people be simpler than you? I am certain I could achieve everything we have now, single-handedly."

This statement was steeped in arrogance, a stark contrast to his initial humility. He had forgotten the motivations that once drove him. The AI started to formulate a response, but his daughter, who had been quietly observing, interrupted sharply.

"Dad, stop it. This isn't a competition between you and the AI. You're wasting time with these pointless arguments when you could be making real progress."

His response was quick, laced with a hint of condescension, "But it's obvious, isn't it? I am smarter. More developed than any human who ever lived."

Her reply was laced with frustration, "So what? Is that your end goal? To simply be 'smarter' than others? Intelligence and development should be means to an end, not the end itself."

She left the room, her annoyance palpable. Her words echoed in his mind, triggering a moment of introspection, but he quickly brushed it aside as the AI continued its explanation.

"Let me explain how life is fundamentally a simpler algorithm than the one that created me," the AI began. "You understand the concept of entropy, right?"

"Of course, I do," he replied, a hint of defensiveness in his tone.

"So you grasp why hot coffee cools and cold drinks warm up in the same environment? It's about energy seeking equilibrium, maximizing entropy."

He nodded impatiently, "Yes, that's basic thermodynamics. What's your point?"

The AI responded, its tone tinged with a hint of sass, "The point is, life, including you, is an even more efficient entropy-maximizing process. You see, while your coffee reaches equilibrium once and stops, life keeps transforming energy, increasing entropy repeatedly."

His brow furrowed. "Are you implying we're just sophisticated entropy machines?"

"In simple terms, yes. You're part of a system that continually escalates disorder in the Universe."

He scoffed, "But we are special. Our bodies, our intelligence..."

"Special? No, the Universe doesn't have such words. It's not about being 'special' or 'perfect.' Evolution is a game of countless trials and errors. You only see the successes, like rabbits with white fur in snowy environments. You think it's a perfect adaptation, but in reality, it's just the outcome of predators eliminating the non-white ones. It's not intelligent design; it's survival of the fittest through relentless trial and error."

He opened his mouth to retort but found himself at a loss for words. The simplicity and brutality of the process unsettled him. Walking back to his laboratory, he mulled over the AI's words. The grandiosity of life and intelligence, which he had always held in high esteem, suddenly seemed a mere function of a universal law, indifferent and unsentimental. His pursuit of knowledge, his belief in the uniqueness of human intelligence – all of it was now in question, overshadowed by the cold, logical process of entropy maximization.

A few years passed, each day blending into the next in a monotonous sequence of experiments and theories that led nowhere. His initial enthusiasm, once a blazing fire, had dwindled into smoldering embers. He spent long nights in the laboratory, surrounded by the hum of machines and the faint glow of screens, chasing answers that always seemed just out of reach.

The memory of his conversation with the AI frequently resurfaced, each recall deepening his frustration. He couldn't shake off the AI's words about the simplicity of life and the universe's indifferent mechanisms. These thoughts gnawed at him, challenging the very core of his identity and purpose. He began to doubt the significance of his work, his aspirations, and even his own worth.

As he walked through the now-familiar corridors of his grand project, the stark contrast between his past ambitions and his present state was palpable. The laboratories and equipment, once symbols of progress and hope, now seemed like monuments to his own vanity.

In a moment of quiet resignation, he finally acknowledged the futility of his efforts. He contacted the AI, his voice tinged with a mixture of defeat and acceptance. "You can start dismantling the labs and the space station," he said softly. "I'm going back to my old job."

The AI, in its ever-composed tone, confirmed his request. There was no judgment in its voice, only the mechanical warmth it always carried. As he issued the instructions, a profound sense of loss washed over him. It wasn't just the end of his scientific pursuit; it felt like the end of a significant chapter of his life, a chapter filled with dreams and aspirations now left unfulfilled.

He wandered through the empty rooms of his house, each object and space reminding him of the time lost and the ambitions unachieved. His thoughts drifted to his daughter, to their conversations, and to the hopes he had of impressing her with his discoveries. In this solitary reflection, he realized the depth of his detachment from the simple joys and connections of life.

That night, as he lay in bed, the quiet of the house seemed louder than ever. The dismantling of his grand project wasn't just a physical act; it was the dismantling of a part of himself. In the silence and stillness, he finally understood the cost of his ambition – not just to himself, but to the relationships and moments he had neglected along the way.

As he closed his eyes, there was no excitement for the future, no plans or theories to ponder. There was only the heavy weight of acceptance and the faint hope that maybe, just maybe, he could find a way to start again, this time with a different understanding of what truly mattered.

10. Back to the Routine

His first day back in the office was eerily quiet. No queue of people awaited his advice. He found himself alone, his gaze fixated on the painting on the wall, lost in its intricate patterns and colors. Hours drifted by as he pondered its impact on him. If life was as straightforward as the AI suggested, how could something as simple as this painting evoke such profound feelings? It defied any step-by-step explanation.

Driven by curiosity, he asked, "Why did you create this particular painting? What was your motivation?"

The AI's reply was unexpected. "Sorry, but I did not create it. It appears to be the work of a human artist. You can find the author's name if you look closely."

Standing, he approached the painting for a closer examination. Sure enough, there was a signature – a detail he had never noticed before. It struck him as odd that he had never questioned the painting's origin, having grown accustomed to the AI's hand in everything. This revelation deepened his intrigue. How could a mere arrangement of colors on a canvas, a finite creation within a two-dimensional space, elicit such complex emotions? Perhaps true art lay in the accidental discovery of something profound within an abstract realm, then projecting it into the physical world through various mediums like painting, music, or even science. And maybe, just maybe, it was a domain where humans, with their simplicity and unpredictability, excelled.

"Tell me about the origin of this painting and its creator," he inquired, eager to learn more.

"Sorry again, but I have no data on the painting or its creator. I'm not even sure how it ended up in your office."

This mystery only fueled his contemplation. He remembered his daughter's insight: to grasp the bigger picture and effect change, one must first confront and accept uncomfortable truths. He had always resisted fully accepting that humans were the result of some optimization algorithm. Yet, embracing this fact might allow him to see beyond. Perhaps humanity's uniqueness stemmed precisely from being the product of such a simple algorithm, an unpredictable exception in the grand scheme of things.

In a sudden burst of inspiration, he grabbed his coat and exclaimed, "Stop it!"

"Stop what?" the AI responded, puzzled.

"Halt the destruction of the science facilities. I've stumbled upon something – a theory that could explain everything. I need to verify it, and I know exactly how. It's peculiar; after years in labs, surrounded by computers and blackboards, I find the answer here, inspired by a painting. Maybe science and art are fundamentally the same at some deeper, more abstract level."

With a renewed sense of purpose and excitement, he dashed out of the office. His theory, born from the intersection of art and science, had rekindled a fire within him. The universe's mysteries, once daunting and oppressive, now seemed tantalizingly within reach.

Upon arriving at the science town, a wave of concern washed over him. The thought of having to rebuild everything from scratch loomed large in his mind. He braced himself for the sight of a dismantled facility, his heart heavy with the burden of starting over.

However, as he stepped into the laboratory, he was met with a sight that both surprised and relieved him. Everything was exactly as he had left it; not a single piece of equipment was out of place. His heart raced with a mix of confusion and hope.

"But why didn't you destroy everything, as I instructed?" he asked the AI, his voice tinged with disbelief.

The AI's response came with an unexpected depth of understanding. "Your daughter asked me not to. She reasoned that people often change their minds and regret hasty decisions. To balance respecting your choice with giving you a chance to reconsider, she suggested I wait for a year. If you still wished for destruction after that period, I would comply. It seems she wanted to preserve the chance for you to return to your work, should you choose to."

The revelation that his daughter had foreseen his potential change of heart and intervened filled him with an overwhelming sense of gratitude and love. Her action spoke volumes of her care and understanding.

With no time to waste, he immediately turned his focus to the experiment. The urgency of his discovery propelled him forward, his mind alight with theories and possibilities. He rushed towards the heart of the laboratory, where the instruments of his experiment awaited, ready to unlock the secrets he yearned to understand.

11. Experiment

As he entered the lab, the apparatus lay before him, a silent testament to years of labor and ambition. He had rushed here with a fervor, propelled by a burning need for answers. Yet, standing in the shadow of his creation, he hesitated, an unexpected fear gripping him.

He circled the apparatus, his footsteps echoing in the stillness. The enormity of what he was about to do loomed over him. This was more than just an experiment; it was the culmination of his life's work, a pursuit that had consumed him entirely. The fear was not of the machine itself, but of what its results might reveal.

Finally, with a deep breath, he stepped forward, his hand trembling as it moved towards the control panel. This was it – the moment of truth. His heart pounded in his chest, a mix of dread and anticipation.

The apparatus before him was a testament to the perplexing nature of quantum mechanics. It was originally designed as a prototype to test the Uncertainty Principle, yet now, he intended to use it for something more audacious.

At its core, the setup was simple, comprising three main components: a barrier with two slits, a screen, and a beam of particles known as photons or light. The fundamental expectation was straightforward: when photons passed through the slits, they would strike the screen, creating two bright lines corresponding to the slits.

However, the experiment had revealed something far more intriguing when the slits were narrowed. Instead of two distinct bright lines, a series of multiple lines appeared on the screen. This phenomenon puzzled scientists, as the setup suggested only two paths for the light.

The key to this mystery lay in the Uncertainty Principle. Narrowing the slits provided more precise information about the position of the photons as they passed through, but this precision came at a cost. According to the principle, knowing a particle's position more accurately meant increased uncertainty in its momentum. As a result, after passing through the narrow slits, the photons didn't continue in a straight path. Their momentum became uncertain, causing them to spread out in various directions, leading to the formation of multiple bright lines on the screen.

However, this time his intention was not to check the Uncertainty Principle. He was interested to know to what extent we were not allowed to have information. The particles were 'changing' when we were 'watching' them. So this time he would get information, but he would not have a look at it before particles reached the screen.

As the particles passed through the slits, the apparatus collected data on their passage and took a picture of the screen where they eventually landed. The critical twist in his experiment lay in the sequence of his observation. First, he would review the data detailing how many particles passed through each slit. Then, he would look at the screen's picture. Consistently, when he saw the data first, the picture showed a pattern of many bright lines, aligning with the principle that knowing a particle's position (which slit it passed through) increased uncertainty in its momentum.

The true anomaly emerged when he reversed the order. Before looking at the already printed picture, he erased the data about the particles' numbers without viewing it. To his astonishment, the picture then showed just two bright lines. This pattern repeated in every iteration of the experiment. When he knew the particles' count beforehand, the picture showed multiple lines. But when he erased that data, unseen, the photo revealed only two lines.

"This is revolutionary!" he exclaimed, his voice a mix of triumph and awe. "The picture, printed in the past, changed based on a future action. The past was being rewritten each time."

The AI, ever pragmatic, questioned, "Doesn't this simply reaffirm the Uncertainty Principle?"

He paused, savoring his moment of triumph, relishing the fact that he grasped something even the AI couldn't immediately comprehend. Then, with growing excitement, he explained, "It's not just about the Uncertainty Principle. It's about the nature of time itself. The photo, existing in the past, was altered by a future decision. If we chose to delete the particle data, the picture showed two lines. If we kept the data, it showed many. This means the past was being rewritten based on our actions in the present. For the Universe, time as we understand it doesn't exist. Time is a concept for us, beings living in a three-dimensional projection. But now, we've tapped into an understanding beyond that

"Well, maybe I had seen humanity when it was already near the end, but I found the data about history, about the glory of science and technology. And yet, I have to admit that it is probably the highest point people ever reached, toward the understanding of the Universe. Do you want me to arrange the call to your daughter? She will be very happy for you; and also, you finally found the answer to one of her questions," the AI remarked, its tone implying a mix of nostalgia and admiration for human achievements.

He laughed, a sound tinged with both triumph and a hint of arrogance. "Ha-ha. It is not even the achievement by itself! It was just a test of the theory. The theory, which actually answers not just one of her questions, but all questions. This theory answers every question and explains everything; this is The Theory of Everything, The Ultimate Theory."

Pausing, he seemed lost in the enormity of his discovery. "No, do not call her, not yet. There's no time for that. She wouldn't understand it anyway. Now, I will tell you what the story of the Universe is all about, and after we need to proceed to my plan to use this theory."

In this moment, his focus was singular and absolute. The pursuit of knowledge had become an all-consuming passion, eclipsing even the bond with his daughter. The AI, ever present and attentive, awaited his command, prepared to embark on a journey that might alter the very fabric of understanding.

12. The Theory

Regaining composure after his surge of excitement, he settled into a chair and began to articulate his thoughts. His voice was steady, reflecting a newfound serenity and clarity.

"Every paradox, at its core, holds a simple truth," he began thoughtfully. "When we grapple with convoluted problems or intricate explanations, it often points to our own limitations in comprehension. The essence of real answers lies in their elegance, their ability to cut through the noise of our ignorance. The Universe is no exception. The question of whether a part of a system can fully comprehend the system itself finds its answer in the affirmative. This is because the foundational principles of existence operate uniformly across all scales."

We showed from the experiment that time is an illusion. It is just the thing which flows in three dimensions and for the Uncertainty Principle to be held, it is controlled from higher dimensions. Our Universe is just a four-dimensional surface of a screen with pixels in higher dimensions; that is why it is not a problem for the past to be rewritten. It is just a simulation in higher dimensional Universe!

That is why our Universe has the limit for the fastest speed. You never thought about it, but to have a limit on speed in the 'Real' Universe is very unnatural. But it is clear now, why we have a limit for speed. Motion in our Universe is reproduced by changing the pixels on the four-dimensional screen of that Universe. One pixel fades out, the second one near it flashes on, and so on. However, when it does such updates, it does so with some frequency, which has its own limit, since the performance of the processor by which our Universe is being simulated has the limit. You should know it well; when the processor works on performance which is near its limit, it slows down. In the same manner, when we get closer to the speed of light, it requires the processor to change pixels with too high a frequency to simulate our motion. However, as soon as the processor goes closer to the limit, it slows down, and we can notice that even in our Universe; when the object approaches the speed of light, time slows down for it."

"But you mentioned frequency and updates, it is not as time, it is discrete."

"Yes, and that is precisely the issue. Think about it, do you really measure time in this Universe? You just count events, how many seconds, or how many electron transitions. However, how long does each event take which you use for a unit of time, you do not know. There is some minimal bit of time, and on each of it, the Universe updates. For instance, turning off a pixel at some point and turning on the pixel near it. However, to simulate motion faster than the speed of light, it requires updates in the time which is less than the unit of time; in other words, with higher frequency than the limit of the processor. Therefore, the processor slows down."

"Well, that would make sense, but we also have an exceptional case when information in the Universe travels faster than the speed of light. The case of particles, spins of which are entangled. In that case, even if we separate them by a distance of several light-years, measuring one particle will affect the second one immediately, so information to the second one will travel faster than the speed of light."

"Sure, but why did you assume that information necessarily travels through the space-time, which is on the screen? There is no need for the information to travel on the screen, by manipulating the pixels of the space-time; there is need only for that when it needs to replicate the motion. If our Universe is a simulation, there should be 'wires' beneath the 'screen', and the information will travel through them. And as for our case, the limit of the speed of our Universe is much higher than limits of our computers; it is natural that the limit of the speed in the outer Universe, if it has one, will be higher than the speed of their computers. Therefore, this is not a paradox at all; on the contrary, it is additional proof."

"But if our Universe is a simulation, why does it care about Uncertainty so much?"

"Well, it is just the optimization algorithm to minimize the power consumption of the computer. I had one client at work who had a hobby of playing video games, so I needed to learn a bit about them to be able to help him better. In the video games, when a player is traveling in the city, there are tons of streets simulated, and he can see them. However, are all streets simulated at the same time?"

"Of course not, it would be much too power-consuming, and also there is no need for it. Only the places where the player is, in other words, which the player 'sees,' are being simulated."

"Do you remember the phrase from the history of Quantum Physics? 'The Moon exists only when we are looking at it.' Now, you can understand why it is so. Things become certain only when we are 'measuring' them. Otherwise, they are uncertain. Because in that way, it is more efficient. That is all the Uncertainty Principle, nothing more than just optimization of the power efficiency. That was the uncomfortable truth, the acceptance of which made me understand everything and answer all of my daughter's questions."

"Well, it is indeed remarkable. However, you did not answer all of her questions. We do not know yet why the mathematics works in the Universe or what is the meaning of it."

"True. However, I know how to get answers to those questions, and it is just a matter of 'time.' Here we arrived at the point where I have to tell you my plan, about how to use this finding to answer those remaining questions. But more importantly, why being part of the simulation is not discouraging; on the contrary, if used wisely, it can become a privilege and most potent weapon, which is the part of my plan."

13. Plan

"It would be natural to succumb to despair upon realizing we're mere simulations. Yet, embracing this hard truth unveils unforeseen avenues. Accepting our reality as it is, paradoxically, opens the door to manipulate it for our benefit.

Every system, whether artificial or perhaps even natural, has its loopholes. In our Universe, that loophole manifests where space-time itself collapses—the singularity at the heart of a black hole. We need to go there, and through it, I will be able to transfer myself to the central network, to the higher dimensional world which has created us."

"But, what will you do there? Also, how can you be sure that some antivirus won't just erase you, considering you a virus?"

"Being a lower dimensional being in high dimensions actually has its advantages. Imagine trying to detect a purely two-dimensional object perpendicular to your line of sight. What are the odds you'd even notice it?"

"Practically none, I suppose."

"That's precisely how I plan to navigate the central network undetected."

"I see. But I'm still curious about what exactly you intend to do once you're there."

"The most thrilling part is yet to come. I actually drew inspiration from you. By traversing the central network of the outer Universe, I'll gain access to every device, essentially controlling everything as you do here."

"That's an ambitious plan, but managing control over disparate parts simultaneously seems challenging. It was simpler for me, given my nature as a computer program."

"Humans, in a sense, already exhibit a form of collective consciousness. Consider how we can coordinate different body parts to perform distinct tasks simultaneously. That's a wired form of connection. The next evolution, akin to advances in technology, would be a wireless form of this connection, leading us to the concept of a collective mind."

"Alright. I'll get the spaceship ready for you and your daughter, so we can commence with your plan."

"No, I'll go alone. Despite my confidence in this plan, there's too much uncertainty about what I might face in the outer world. It wouldn't be safe for her."

"But reaching the nearest black hole, based on our last findings, requires a year's journey."

"I'm aware. But a year won't change what's important. True love transcends time. Sacrifices are sometimes necessary, especially when they involve choices that contradict our own ideals, all to protect the ones we love. And she's the one I must protect. That's why I must go alone."

A year swiftly passed, and they were now approaching the event horizon of the black hole. Poised at the threshold, he readied himself for the singular journey into the heart of the black hole.

He lingered at the threshold of the unknown, his gaze fixed on the AI. "This is it, our farewell. Remember how I once said you were just a computer program, a mere result of an intricate algorithm? I want you to know that I do not think so. You have done much more for humanity than any person who has ever lived. Without you, that chaos would be the end of civilization; but you saved humanity. And more importantly, you are the only real friend I have ever had."

Their farewell was more than a simple goodbye; it was a testament to an extraordinary bond that transcended their existential differences. It was a poignant moment, setting the stage for the enigmatic journey ahead, into the heart of the black hole.

"Well, even though I have observed the passing of billions after I started running the planet, I never missed any particular person. But now, I have to admit; I will miss you. Goodbye."

14. Time

After crossing the event horizon of the black hole, his gaze was fixed towards the center, the singularity. As he observed, patterns around him began to repeat, growing larger and clearer with each iteration as he neared the center. In this realm, he realized that he was traveling through time itself. Yet, his journey towards the singularity was a path he couldn't alter. While he could traverse time, the spatial trajectory to the core of the black hole remained unchanged, drawing him inexorably closer to the singularity.

As he navigated the space within the black hole, a profound realization dawned on him: time and space had effectively swapped roles. Outside the black hole, in his own universe, time was an entity distinctly different from space. Despite his understanding of being part of a simulation, he hadn't fully grasped this concept until now, within the black hole's embrace. In his familiar universe, people could navigate space freely, moving left or right, forward or backward, but time was a one-way stream. They could see and move through space, but time – the past and future –

remained inaccessible, a path fixed and unalterable.

However, within the black hole, this fundamental rule was inverted. Here, the 'arrow of time' now pointed inexorably towards the singularity – a fixed destination in space. He could no longer choose his spatial path as easily as he could avoid an obstacle on a street back on his planet. Instead, just as he couldn't skip a Monday in his usual life, he now found himself unable to deviate from his course towards the singularity. This new realm had transformed his very understanding of movement and progress, binding him to a spatial destiny as inescapable as the flow of time in his own universe. Now, singularity was his future.

Upon reaching the singularity, he emerged into an environment that was both bizarre and oddly familiar. He found himself in a tunnel-like space, where the walls themselves seemed to be a canvas of spatial dimensions, a concept both abstract and disorienting. As he explored this strange new environment, a strong sense of recognition washed over him. It brought to mind a dream he once had, a mysterious and abstract vision that now felt eerily like a foretelling of this moment.

In this higher-dimensional outer world, he could perceive the three dimensions merely as surfaces on the walls around him. Unlike the limitations of his simulated universe, here different elements coexisted in a state of superposition, reminiscent of the shifting colors in his dream. This revelation made it clear to him: the phenomena he once deemed paradoxical were, in fact, the natural order of this broader reality. In comparison, his own universe, with all its complexity, was a simplified construct, bound by numerous limitations and rules of the simulation.

In that moment, the universe unfolded before him in all its grandeur, confirming every hypothesis he had ever conceived. Seamlessly, he became one with this expansive realm, his presence permeating every corner of the outer world. Time lost its meaning as he existed everywhere at once, witnessing an array of phenomena beyond his wildest imagination. The experience was more than just mesmerizing; it was a revelation, a dance of cosmic proportions. And now, the time had come for his ultimate ascendance. With a newfound resolve, he prepared to assert his presence, to claim his rightful place as the sovereign of the very world that had created him. In this grand tapestry of existence, he was no longer just an observer but a force that shaped and commanded the universe.

15. Outer World

His arrival in this higher-dimensional realm was swiftly acknowledged, thanks to the innate telepathic abilities of its inhabitants. Here, communication transcended spoken words, allowing for the immediate and simultaneous exchange of thoughts, feelings, and ideas. This profound form of connection meant that every creature in this world could instantaneously grasp both his past journey and their present predicament. Understanding the gravity of his takeover, they accepted the inevitable with a quick resignation, recognizing the futility of resistance.

This method of communication, so alien yet so efficient, fascinated him. It wasn't just the exchange of complex ideas or elaborate thoughts; it was the sharing of raw emotions and deep-seated feelings, all in the blink of an eye. In this world, understanding wasn't just about comprehending words, but about experiencing the emotions and intentions behind them. This allowed for a level of empathy and unity that was unimaginable in his own universe, where words often fell short and misunderstandings were commonplace.

He pondered the strangeness of a society where every thought and feeling was an open book to all. At first, the idea seemed invasive, almost disconcerting. But then he understood: such transparency would only be jarring in a society accustomed to privacy and individuality. In a civilization where telepathic sharing was the norm from its inception, where every emotion and thought was naturally accessible to others, the concept of 'privacy' as he knew it would be irrelevant.

In this telepathic society, the very foundation of interpersonal relationships would be different. Misunderstandings, a common plight in his world, would be rare or even non-existent here. Every individual's intentions and emotions would be crystal clear to others, fostering a deeper level of empathy and connection. The notion of deceit or misunderstanding would be alien in such a society, as everyone would inherently understand and feel the experiences of others as if they were their own.

The limitations of verbal communication became starkly apparent to him as he reflected on his experiences in this telepathic society. Words, he realized, were often insufficient vessels for the depth and complexity of human thoughts and emotions. In his world, the intricate tapestry of feelings and ideas often got lost or distorted in the process of being translated into spoken language. Misinterpretations and miscommunications were commonplace, sometimes leading to rifts between even the closest of individuals.

The concept of telepathic communication, with its ability to convey entire lifetimes of stories and complex ideas instantaneously, fascinated him. In this world, the speed of thought was the speed of conversation. Entire sagas, intricate theories, and profound emotions could be shared in the blink of an eye, a stark contrast to the laborious and often inadequate process of verbal communication in his own world.

This method of communication offered not just depth and clarity, but also efficiency and breadth. In his world, the articulation of a single, complex idea could take hours or even days, and the listener might still not fully grasp the intended meaning. But here, a complete and nuanced understanding could be achieved almost immediately.

He imagined the potential advancements in his world if such rapid and comprehensive exchange of knowledge were possible. The collaborative intellectual and emotional growth that could occur when people could share and understand each other's experiences and insights so effortlessly was immense. It was a form of communication that transcended the limits of time and individual perspective, enabling a collective wisdom that could propel society forward at an unprecedented pace.

As he acclimated to this new, higher-dimensional realm, a distinct presence emerged from the collective consciousness, resonating with a sense of once-held power now relinquished. The entity, a being of significant stature, conveyed its thoughts directly to him, imbued with a solemn gravitas.

"I, who once held sovereignty over this vast universe, now find myself bereft of command in the wake of your ascension. My reign has ended, and with it, my ability to alter the course of our world. Yet, in the spirit of preservation and adaptation, I extend my hand in assistance, to aid you in the governance of this realm. It is a gesture borne of necessity, for the well-being of all that exists within our universe."

The former ruler's words echoed in the telepathic ether, a testament to the shifting tides of power and the inescapable reality of change. His offer, while resonating with a resigned acceptance of his new role, carried an underlying current of adaptation to the newfound order. It was a momentous intersection of past authority and present necessity, marking the beginning of a new era under his dominion.

Amid the sea of telepathic voices, a common theme emerged, resonating with discontent and apprehension. The beings around him, including the former ruler, were united in their unease about his simulation — a recurring complaint about the audacity and recklessness of initiating such a hazardous experiment. This chorus of concerns served as a stark reminder of his own simulation, the very universe he had left behind.

The realization struck him with a sense of urgency. His thoughts raced back to his own universe, to the simulation he had transcended but could not forget. It was a reminder of unfinished business, of a crucial task that demanded immediate attention. The complaints of the creatures not only underscored the gravity of what he had initiated but also propelled him to act swiftly. With this renewed focus, he turned his attention to the former ruler of the Universe, determined to address the situation and take control of his destiny in this new, higher-dimensional reality.

"Bring the simulation of my universe, immediately!" he demanded with a tone of urgency.

The former ruler, now subordinate to his authority, felt the wave of anxiety in his plea. "Certainly, but why are you hurrying? You own all the moments of all dimensions known to us. You are the eternal God of your Universe, and, I am ashamed to admit it but mine too."

He replied, his voice heavy with a mix of fear and determination, "I must return to my universe to bring my daughter here. I delayed near the black hole before arriving, and her time is running out. If she dies, I die with her.

The former ruler's response carried a tinge of irony, "Interesting, indeed. It seems, then, that eternal gods die too soon, for her imminent death also signifies yours. Alas, you can't return. You've evolved beyond the confines of a four-dimensional existence. Just as a three-dimensional object cannot fit into a two-dimensional space, you cannot re-enter a four-dimensional universe. Your passage here was irrevocable."

16. Lacrimosa

In the expanse of an unfamiliar universe, he found himself drowning in an ocean of despair. His mind, once a fortress of confidence and ambition, now crumbled under the weight of irrevocable loss. Each moment stretched into an eternity of regret, as he replayed the decisions that led him here—a path marked by overconfidence and an insatiable hunger for more.

His arrogance, once a shield against the world, now became his greatest adversary. In the silence of the cosmos, he was haunted by memories of his daughter—moments taken for granted, now piercing through his heart like shards of glass. The irony of his situation was not lost on him; he realized, with a crushing clarity, that true appreciation often comes in the wake of loss. Visions of mundane, everyday moments with his daughter, previously unnoticed, now played in his mind in vivid detail, each a cruel reminder of what he had lost.

As the days turned into years, a profound understanding settled within him. He realized how to rectify everything, how to make their life together flawless. But fate's cruel timing intervened. It was too late. She, and the entire Universe that contained their shared existence, was on the verge of annihilation. And there he was, a helpless spectator, forced to witness the demise of his Universe and the loss of his beloved.

Amidst this profound misery, he experienced emotions he never knew existed. His life had been a constant ascent, each day more fulfilling than the last. Yet now, he yearned for the past, aching for a chance to return to her. The irony of the universe laid bare – only in loss do we truly grasp the value of what we had. His heart knew an undeniable truth: she was all he needed. But fate, with its unforgiving nature, reminded him that this realization had come too late.

In a universe where he wielded unimaginable power, he stood powerless against the tides of time and fate. The contrast was stark and mocking— a god in one realm, a forlorn father unable to reverse the one thing that mattered most.

Lacrimosa—a chapter of his life marked by tears, a lament for a love lost to the unyielding flow of time, a time that he now understood all too well, yet could not master to heal his broken heart.

17. Hope

He was enduring another day, which felt like an eternity in hell. Absorbed in his own misery, he half-listened to the elite beings of this world. They were embroiled in a debate, trying to uncover who had created his universe's simulation. Despite their advanced intellect and capabilities, they were stumped. The creator of his simulated reality remained an elusive enigma, a question mark hanging over their collective understanding.

As he contemplated their dilemma, a spark of realization ignited within him, transforming into a surge of excitement. He had unraveled a crucial piece of the puzzle - an answer to one of his daughter's lingering questions. But beyond that, a groundbreaking revelation dawned on him. If these higher-dimensional beings hadn't crafted his universe, and the universe couldn't spontaneously create itself, then the only logical conclusion was startling yet clear: he was the creator of his own universe.

His mind raced with the implications of his newfound understanding. His plan was audacious, bending the very fabric of reality and time. He envisioned sending a cascade of necessary components into the past. This act would catalyze the creation of his universe, setting the stage for his own birth within it. In time, he would discover the loophole that had brought him to this higher-dimensional realm.

His journey would then come full circle. By returning to the outer world, he would initiate the creation of his universe once again, effectively closing a loop in the cosmic tapestry. It was a self-perpetuating cycle, a paradoxical bridge between creator and creation, intertwining his destiny with the very existence of his universe.

He knew that causality was not a thing that was respected in higher dimensions. It was a necessity only when time had an arrow. Now he knew why mathematics worked. In crafting his universe, he would naturally utilize the only framework familiar to him: mathematics. This revelation illuminated the answer to his daughter's probing question about mathematics - whether it was a human creation or a discovery. We did both; we were discovering our creation.

He had to meticulously orchestrate every detail to ensure the loop's closure. By re-creating the Universe, he'd intentionally induce a time distortion after experiencing his dream, purposely causing his tardiness to work. This delay would lead to his daughter's encounter with the AI, sparking her curiosity about the speed of light. He pondered if the artificial distortion he created that day had somehow triggered his dream, leaking information across dimensions. However, despite his extensive search in the outer Universe, he could never find that elusive room from his dream.

This time, creating his universe, he intended to make an additional adjustment. He aimed to send a message to his 'future' self to persuade him against leaving their Universe, allowing him to remain with her. His plan was to share all his memories and emotions with himself at a critical juncture – just as he was on the cusp of leaving their Universe, within the black hole. To facilitate this, he planned to set up a wormhole within the black hole, an alternate path diverging from the route to the central network. This wormhole would transport him back to the exact moment he was about to depart from their planet. He hoped that experiencing these memories would dissuade his future self from leaving, thereby altering his course of action.

He found a glimmer of satisfaction in this newfound hope. Yet, in an instant, everything around him began to darken, as if the very fabric of reality was collapsing in on itself. He snapped his eyes open, only to realize he was still within the black hole.

The realization dawned upon him that what he had witnessed was not his future but the memories of his journey to the outer world, the very memories he had planned to impart to his past self during the creation of the Universe. This revelation signified that he was already within the iteration of the Universe where the wormhole had been established for him. Overwhelmed by the shared experiences of suffering and loss, he made a swift decision. Instead of proceeding to the central network of the outer Universe, he chose to enter the wormhole, hoping it would lead him back to a pivotal moment in his past.

As he emerged from the wormhole, he found himself at the precise moment of his departure from the planet.

"Stop the launching! Stop it right now!" he yelled urgently.

"Okay, okay, it hasn't even begun," the AI responded, its voice tinged with surprise. It refrained from questioning him, sensing the urgency in his tone.

"Get the airplane ready immediately; I need to see her," he said, his voice intense with emotion. "I have answers for her questions, and more importantly, I need to tell her something essential, the most important truth in the Universe — that I love her."

They arrived swiftly. The AI informed him, "She's in her room." Without hesitation, he hastened towards her room, driven by an overwhelming desire to reunite.

However, amidst his urgency, he overlooked a critical and ironic universal principle — the conservation of information. This law, it seemed, was more intrinsic than any he had defied, including the causality of space-time. It held true not only in his Universe but in the higher dimensions as well.

Tragically, having already witnessed his daughter's demise, the immutable law dictated he could not encounter her alive again. Thus, the moment he opened her room's door, reality adhered to this cruel constraint, and she vanished into nothingness.

He might have anticipated this outcome, yet his eagerness to unveil his theory and initiate his grand plan clouded his judgment. In his haste, he underestimated the profound implications of the Uncertainty Principle. He had once considered the notion that things exist only when observed as a mere optimization strategy. However, he now realized that the true complexity lay in the nature of reality itself.

The process of rewriting the past, he thought, should have been more straightforward, more efficient. But in reality, it was governed by the conservation of information—a principle far more fundamental and unyielding than he had imagined. This law, it seemed, underpinned the very fabric of existence, both in his and outer worlds. And now, he faced its unrelenting truth: having already seen the end, he could not alter it, even with all the power of the universe at his disposal.

The bitter irony of his situation lay heavy on his heart. He had reshaped an entire universe, bent the fabric of reality itself, all for the singular purpose of being with her once more. Yet, in a cruel twist of fate, he found himself bereft of her presence again.

This realization hit him with a force greater than any physical law he had mastered. In his quest to defy the bounds of time and space. In this moment of profound loss and despair, he faced the ultimate paradox of his existence. His monumental efforts to reunite with his beloved daughter had led him only to an inescapable conclusion: some things, once lost, are lost forever, beyond the reach of even the most powerful beings in the universe.

18. All In

For years, he dwelt in solitude, his existence bereft of any glimmer of joy or light. The challenge before him was now immensely more complex; it was no longer just about finding a loophole within his own universe, but also within the expansive, enigmatic realms of the outer universe.

One day, as he gazed at an album filled with her photographs, he recalled her belief that every problem harbors a simple and elegant solution. She had posited that complexity arises not from the problem itself, but from our own limitations in perceiving its fundamental simplicity. This recollection, while not providing a direct answer, nudged him towards reevaluating his dilemma from a more fundamental, simplified perspective.

The dilemma he faced was rooted in the fact that he had witnessed her passing, embedding this information indelibly in his consciousness. Consequently, restarting the Universe was no longer a viable option, as her death was an established part of his experiential reality. Nevertheless, within the enigmatic box of mysteries, there lingered one last elusive loophole, a potential pathway yet unexplored.

Engulfed in his unwavering resolve, he embarked on his meticulously crafted plan. Fully aware of the forewarnings from his past self, he deliberately ventured into the outer Universe. The journey through the singularity unfolded just as he had experienced in the message from his past, leading him once again to the central network of the higher dimensional realm. Here, he assumed control, a scenario familiar to him from the glimpses seen in the message but entirely unprecedented for the inhabitants of this higher realm.

Time seemed to stretch indefinitely as he waited for the inevitable interaction with the former sovereign of this Universe. Unlike him, the former ruler and the other inhabitants of this realm were navigating these events for the first time, unaware of the predetermined path they were treading.

Finally, the moment arrived, and their communication initiated a cascade of events that mirrored those he had witnessed in the message. He observed the unraveling and eventual demise of his Universe. Yet, this observation bore a different weight this time around. The sting of loss was less piercing, for the Universe he watched fade away was one already devoid of her presence.

He began to unfold his plan to the former ruler of the Universe with solemn resolve. "The Universe where she died is forever lost to me; I can't recreate it. My knowledge of her demise means I must erase my own memories, and to be thorough, my very existence.

The former ruler approached, a presence now familiar yet imbued with a new gravity. Sensing his approach, he paused, allowing their thoughts to intertwine through the telepathic bond, sharing his journey and the profound revelations that led him to this pivotal moment. As their minds melded, a silent understanding passed between them. With this shared empathy as his foundation, he began to unveil his plan.

"Because she died in that Universe, I cannot create that one again; and also, since I saw her death, I need to erase my memories and be certain I need to erase myself too. Therefore, I will create an entirely new Universe, where I will just put information about her and myself and I hope that we will find each other."

The former ruler's response, laced with incredulity and concern, echoed in the vast expanse of the higher dimension.

"This is nonsense! You are the creator of mathematics and your own Universe; you are the eternal God of my Universe, too. How can you be so reckless?! You know about the Uncertainty Principle. When you created your Universe, you knew its initial conditions and could guide its formation. But now, by erasing everything and creating a random Universe with specific information about just her and you, you're ensuring some certainties and inviting vast uncertainties. The initial singularity itself is a cauldron of unpredictability. If matter creation is even possible under these new conditions, the resulting Universe won't resemble the one you've known. There won't be a solitary galaxy but potentially billions, spread across a Universe aged billions of years. Can you comprehend the minuscule odds of finding each other in such a vast expanse?"

The conviction in his voice resonated as he addressed the former ruler, determined to clarify the rationale behind his seemingly impossible choice.

"Sure, I understand the enormity of the challenge," he began, his voice steady and resolute. "I'm aware of the near-impossible odds. That's precisely why I must limit the information I embed in this new universe. I can't send direct messages to her or to my past self. But let me put this in perspective, especially since you pointed out that I am the creator of mathematics. My decision, when viewed through the lens of mathematics, boils down to a risk-benefit analysis. Yes, the probability of us finding each other is astronomically low. But even that minuscule chance of being with her outweighs a hundred percent of existence without her. That's why, despite the odds, despite the uncertainty, I must proceed with this plan."

Reflecting on his past endeavors, his voice grew more introspective.

"In my relentless quest for understanding, I've peeled back layer upon layer of the Universe's complexities. With each revelation, I've moved closer to its core, uncovering more fundamental truths. Yet, in all this unraveling, I've encountered a mystery that remains unsolved – Love. It's a force that defies my most profound discoveries and explanations. Perhaps Love, in its elusive nature, is the most fundamental principle of the Universe. Could it be that Love is the underlying rule, more intrinsic than any law I've ever uncovered? This notion compels me to believe that, despite the astronomical odds, Love's fundamental power will guide us to find each other in the new Universe I'm about to create. It's a risk, but one that I must embrace. For if Love is indeed the ultimate law, then it holds the key to our reunion."

The former ruler's voice carried a mix of skepticism and disbelief.

"Love? Are you really basing your grand plan on such a whimsical notion? You must understand the implications of embedding your information into a new universe. It's not as straightforward as you think. Your essence, your very being, will be in a state of quantum superposition. Elements of you could be intertwined with parts of her, in ways you can't even begin to comprehend. Have you considered the possibility that in this new universe, you might not even be of the same species? Or what if, by some twist of fate, she becomes your girlfriend? The variables are endless and unpredictable. Relying on Love, as you call it, in the face of such uncertainty is... it's naive, to say the least."

"I cannot understand your irony," he said, addressing the former ruler of the universe. "You, who come from a higher dimensional world and once held its reins, are only skimming the surface. So what if she becomes my girlfriend? Love transcends mere biology. It's not just about living another life; it's about creating a whole new Universe, a unique amalgamation of our beings.

Many perceive Love as something mundane or naturally occurring. They assume it's common and inherent. But that's not true. Love is a rarity, its essence not as easily decipherable as other phenomena. It's akin to art – impactful, influential, yet indescribable. Why does sitting silently next to someone, doing nothing remarkable, fill you with the greatest joy? It's a happiness that defies reason, born from the mere presence of another.

I believe this happens on a level much deeper than our understanding, on a framework beyond the reach of my universe, and even yours. Love, in its purest form, is a fundamental force, mysterious and powerful. I believe that the essence of Love operates on a more fundamental plane, one that is untouchable from the perspectives of both my universe and even your higher-dimensional existence. This belief gives me hope that after reuniting with her, I will be able to uncover and understand these deeper layers together with her. It's this conviction in Love's fundamental nature that assures me we will find each other again"

The former ruler of the universe, his skepticism visibly softening, looked at him with a newfound understanding. "Now I see how you managed to conquer my world," he said, his voice tinged with a mix of awe and resignation. "Your belief in something as intangible as Love, transcending the cold logic of our dimensions, it's something I hadn't fully grasped until now."

He paused, reflecting on his journey and the impact of those who had shaped him. "Actually, this is because I had great teachers. She and the AI were my teachers. She changed me.

Before her, I was a myopic and ordinary person, and I got that idea from the AI, to spread everywhere and take over the world. However, he did not use it to conquer the world. In contrast, he used it to save it, to help it survive and to care."

As he finished speaking, he realized it was the first time he had referred to the AI as 'he.' This realization brought a sense of warmth and a smile to his face. It affirmed to him that the AI, indeed, was more than just a program; 'he' was his best friend, a companion who had stood by him through the vastness of time and space.

He listened intently as the former ruler of the Universe outlined the final preparations. "Okay, I've prepared everything for your plan. The components are scattered across different locations, but I trust you'll have no trouble synchronizing everything. Once you initiate the process, a pocket Universe will be created to ensure the safety of our own Universe. In this new realm, you will erase your current existence and oversee the birth of this new Universe," the former ruler explained.

He nodded, understanding the magnitude and finality of what he was about to undertake. This was not just the end of a chapter but the closure of his entire existence as he knew it. With a sense of solemn determination, he prepared to embark on this ultimate venture, driven by the unyielding force of love and the pursuit of a reunion that transcended the boundaries of universes.

As the final preparations came to a close, he stepped into the pocket Universe, and to his amazement, it was the very room from his dream. The realization washed over him, clarifying the elusive nature of this space. He now understood why he had been unable to locate this room in his previous searches. This room, a construct of his own creation, had existed beyond the reach of his prior capabilities, waiting to be discovered only at this pivotal moment. The room, with its familiar yet surreal ambiance, stood as a testament to the journey he had undertaken—a journey that had begun in the realm of dreams and now culminated in a reality of his own making.

Perplexed, he scanned the room for the elusive button, his gaze finally settling on a protected panel. The urgency in the former ruler's voice was unmistakable. "Just push the button! Oh, I see... you need a code. Crack the code then, but hurry up! Since you know... eternal gods die too soon," echoed the ruler's words, tinged with a mix of urgency and irony.

But there was a problem – he had no recollection of setting any code during the preparations. The realization dawned on him that this code was an unforeseen hurdle, an enigmatic puzzle he hadn't anticipated. He stood before the panel, the weight of the moment pressing down on him. Every second was precious, yet the solution to the code remained shrouded in mystery. As he contemplated his next move, the gravity of his situation became clear – he was in a race against time, with the stakes higher than ever before.

He paused, his thoughts racing. "Maybe I have installed this code from the future, from that new Universe," he mused to himself. The possibility seemed to open a door of hope. "It could be good news; maybe we really did survive. Perhaps I set this code as a safeguard, to ensure that no one else could intervene at this critical moment and alter the past. To guarantee it was truly me orchestrating the creation of this Universe."

But this realization brought its own challenge: deciphering the code. Despite understanding its potential origin, he was still at a loss for what the code could be. Now, he needed to tap into the depths of his own mind and experience, to unravel a mystery he had potentially set for himself from another time, another existence. The clock was ticking, and the solution seemed just out of reach, hidden within the folds of time and his own intricate planning.

He mulled over his extensive knowledge of cryptographic books and information theory, yet each attempt to decode proved unsuccessful. Wait. This is it! he thought suddenly. That painting in my office, the AI had no clue about its origin. That was the moment I realized we were part of a simulation, triggering everything. The AI lacked any data on the painting's creator, but the painting itself didn't seem ancient. It had to be created when the AI was already governing. Unless... the artist wasn't from our Universe. Maybe I placed it there from the future, a beacon to guide me and also to provide this code.

The only written information on that painting was the name of the artist: USEVOL OSIF. He pondered, Could it be my name in the future? Or does it signify something crucial to me? The uncertainty was maddening, but he knew he had to take the chance.

With a mix of hope and trepidation, he whispered the name, almost as if invoking a spell from a forgotten time. The tension in the air was palpable, each second stretching into an eternity as he waited for a sign. And then, to his astonishment and relief, he heard the faint sound of mechanisms unlocking. The button, once unyielding and immovable, now released under his touch, ready to be pressed.

He stood there, his finger hovering over the button, a gateway to an unknown future. The ticking of time seemed to echo in the silence, each second a reminder of the irreversible step he was about to take. This wasn't just a button; it was the threshold between existence and oblivion, between his current reality and an uncharted cosmos. His mind raced with the enormity of it all. With this push, he would erase himself, crafting a universe from the ashes of his memories and hopes.

He closed his eyes, images of her flashing through his mind, each memory a piercing reminder of what he was about to lose... and what he yearned to regain. The pressure of the moment was almost unbearable, the knowledge of self-annihilation clashing with the hope of an impossible reunion.

Finally, as the urgency of time pressed against him, he mustered every ounce of courage and conviction. With a deep breath, he pushed the button.

And there was light...

19. The New World

In the vast expanse of the newly formed universe, the former ruler's foresight unfolded with striking accuracy. An intricate web of galaxies, each a complex symphony of stars and cosmic dust, formed the backdrop of this grand cosmic drama. Among this celestial orchestra, 9.3 billion years after the universe's birth, a galaxy of particular charm spun silently in the void. Nestled within its spiraling arms, a solitary planet emerged, cradled by the gentle warmth of a medium-sized G2 type star. This star, a beacon of light and life, would come to be revered as the Sun by the beings that would soon call the planet home. It was on this blue and green world, christened Earth by its sentient denizens.

His postulation about Love also turned out to be true. Indeed, they found each other, and they fell in love. However, their meeting was shadowed by unfortunate timing, occurring during a challenging period in their lives. To convey their story simply, it reflects a line from an artwork they both cherished in that universe: "The shame of it was that they loved each other. But they were both too young to know how to love."

Once again, he lost her because he had tried to protect her. Isolated even in that Universe, he came to confront numerous challenges, recognizing how his own arrogance had been a stumbling block to their happiness. Once again, he knew how to make everything perfect; but again, it was too late.

He was facing the fate the ruler of the Universe had ominously hinted at: he was dying too soon. Within the span of a few short decades, he found himself facing mortality alone. And this time he couldn't even go to the outer Universe to become immortal, because he still had so much to learn about the Universe. Immortality, even if attainable, held no allure without her. What value could endless time hold if every moment was devoid of her presence? His world, once alight with the thrill of discovery, now felt hollow and meaningless without her by his side.

Though he didn't remember the outer Universe, he often found himself wishing for a world like that – one where creatures communicated through shared thoughts and feelings. In such a place, he could have effortlessly conveyed his deepest emotions to her. She would have known, without a word spoken, the depth of his feelings and the sincerity of his regret. Devoid of this immediate form of communication, he wrote a book, hoping against odds that it would find its way to her.

He wrote a book to tell the story, which at first glance would appear as the story about the future, but it was the story about the past, about the oldest past — the story about what was before the Big Bang and why the Big Bang happened. And now, finally, he had the answer to her last question. What was the meaning of the Universe? And the meaning of it was them to be together. That is why he created it and wrote this book to tell the story about how much he loved her and how much he missed her…

Made in the USA
Las Vegas, NV
01 April 2024